The Teachers'
Night Before Christmas

The Teachers' Night Before Christmas

By Steven L. Layne
Illustrated by James Rice

PELICAN PUBLISHING COMPANY
Gretna 2001

For Debbie—my favorite teacher, my partner in all things,
and the one true love of my life.
And with great appreciation to Lynda Moreau for sharing the idea!

The word "Pelican" and the depiction of a pelican are trademarks
of Pelican Publishing Company, Inc.,
and are registered in the U.S. Patent and Trademark Office.

Library of Congress Cataloging-in-Publication Data

Layne, Steven L.
  Teachers' night before Christmas / by Steven L. Layne ; illustrated by James Rice.
    p. cm.
Summary: Exhausted from parties and pageants at school but with presents still to buy, teachers are greeted at the mall by an unexpected helper driving a flying schoolbus.
  ISBN 1-56554-833-7 (hc : alk. paper)
  1. Teachers–Juvenile poetry. 2. Christmas–Juvenile poetry. 3. Santa Claus–Juvenile poetry. 4. Children's poetry, American. [1. Teachers–Poetry. 2. Christmas–Poetry. 3. Santa Claus–Poetry. 4. American poetry.] I. Rice, James, 1934- ill. II. Moore, Clement Clarke, 1779-1863. Night before Christmas. III. Title.
  PS3612.A96 T4 2001
  811'.54–dc21

                                                          2001002106

Printed in Hong Kong

Published by Pelican Publishing Company, Inc.
1000 Burmaster Street, Gretna, Louisiana 70053

THE TEACHERS' NIGHT
BEFORE CHRISTMAS

'Twas the week before Christmas
And all through the town
Every schoolteacher scurried—
They could not slow down.

Their brains were all frazzled
From school celebrations
And the seasonal rush
Of *pre-Christmas* vacation.

The festive art projects,
A yearly tradition,
Had ended as always
In room demolition!

And a nursing-home trip
Earned one principal's pout.
When Pierre pulled the fire alarm,
They cleared the place out!

Then the holiday pageants
Produced minor troubles—
Like the Virgin and Joseph
On stage blowing bubbles.

And then one of God's angels
Got airsick and cried,
"Mrs. Bigler, I've thrown up
On Joe, Tom, and Clyde!"

And unique *Yuletide Bingo,*
Which started out nice,
Until Mike Hattendorf
Won a bingo game *twice!*

Then the other kids hollered
And threw such a fit
That the game was short-lived
Because everyone quit.

But the moms were undaunted.
They moved on to crafts
With some glue guns and scissors
And spray paint and masks.

And inside of one hour
The *ten-minute* wreaths
Were lying all over
And drying on sheets.

Then the students and mothers
Departed the school,
And the teachers rushed home—
Just a few days 'til yule!

With a tree still to trim,
Christmas candy to make,
The cards yet to mail,
Plus a fruitcake to bake.

So when Christmas Eve came
They were all feeling blue,
For the teachers still had
Christmas *shopping* to do!

Thus, they started at once
To converge on the mall,
But the sight of a school bus
In flight stopped them all!

SOUTHSIDE MALL

It was jolly St. Nick
Steering down from the sky
In a sport coat (suede elbows),
New glasses, and tie.

He was quite the professor—
And his class looked "in session"
With a busload of elves
Far too busy to question.

He'd assigned them the task
Of creating a toy
That not even a child like
Ben Grey could destroy!

When he stepped off the bus
All the teachers felt fine—
Then he opened a grade book
And said, "Get in line.

"Mrs. Bigler, Miss Haley,
Miss Elks, Mr. Best,
Mrs. Bruni, Ms. Jance,
Dr. Johns, and the rest!

"You've been working so hard
For your students, I've seen,
That you've run short on time
For your own Christmas scene."

"I've been checking my records
Throughout this past year
And your grades indicate
That you've nothing to fear!

"Santa truly loves teachers,
Support staff, and such.
Your students are blessed
'Cause you've given so much."

"So I'm telling you all
And your colleagues here, too,
Stop this last-minute shopping—
I'll take care of you!

"Go on home. Get to bed.
Leave the *Big Guy* in charge!
I'll take care of those wish lists
No matter how large."

NORTH POLE

Then he beeped the bus horn
While he stepped on the gas,
And he gave a soft laugh
As his bus flew on past.

"Merry Christmas to all!"
His voice rang out with might.
"But *especially* to teachers
And especially *tonight!*"